For Savvy,

You'll always be my little princess.

All my love,
Daddy

Designed by Flowerpot Press
www.FlowerpotPress.com
DJS-1209-0190 ∗ 978-1-4867-1823-8
Made in China/Fabriqué en Chine

MY BIG LITTLE GIRL

A Book for Dads and Daughters

Written by Greg Pope   Illustrated by Lea Wells

A little girl came into the world
and captured her daddy's heart.

She held it there in her gentle hands
right from the very start.

He watched her grow, learn to crawl,
then stand up tall to walk.

And in no time this little girl
would talk, talk, talk, talk, talk...

She loved to play, spin in her dress,
and laugh, and dance, and sing.

This precious girl loved all the world
and every living thing.

And soon this independent girl
would do so much on her own.

Except the thing her dad had done
since the day he brought her home.

With big strong arms he would pick her up
and whisk her off to bed.

Then gently lay her down to sleep
and sweetly kiss her head.

No matter what, this always was
his favorite time of day.

When he held her softly in his arms,
the world would melt away.

And then one night it happened...

His daughter had grown tired
and said, "Dad, it's time for bed."

So he swooped in and picked her up
and threw her overhead.

But his little girl then spoke the words
that filled his heart with fear.

It was an unexpected sentence
that he didn't want to hear.

"Daddy, I'm a big girl.
You don't have to carry me.

Put me down. I can do it.
Just watch, and you will see."

"I'm not scared. I won't fall.
I don't need any help.

Dad, I am a big girl now
and can do this by myself."

And so he stood and watched her go
just like his girl had asked.

And with each stair his daughter climbed,
his mind was racing fast.

He thought of all that she would do,
everywhere that she would go.

Of all the things that lay ahead
and the world she'd come to know.

But then he heard from up the stairs
a voice call down to him.

"Come on, Daddy! Hurry up!
Are you going to tuck me in?"

So up he ran to tuck her in,
all snuggled in her bed.

He leaned in close to hug her tight
and gently kiss her head.

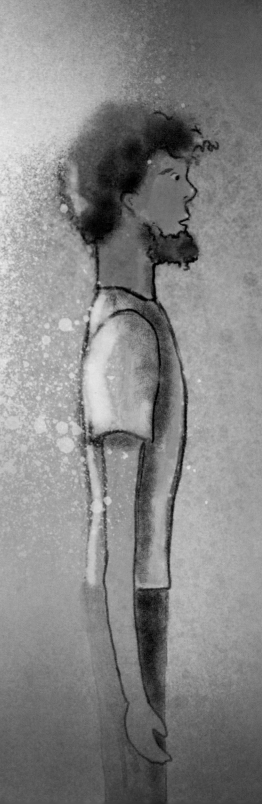

She's a big girl now, her daddy thought,
and getting bigger every day.

But she will always be my daughter.
That will never go away.